TALES FROM GOLD MOUNTAIN

TALES FROM
GOLD MOUNTAIN

Stories of the Chinese
in the New World

BY
Paul Yee

PAINTINGS BY
Simon Ng

Macmillan Publishing Company
New York

Macmillan Publishing Company
866 Third Avenue, New York, NY 10022

Originally published by Groundwood Books,
Toronto, Canada

First American Edition

10 9 8 7 6 5 4 3 2

Library of Congress Cataloging-in-Publication Data

Yee, Paul,
Tales from Gold Mountain.

Summary: A collection of eight stories reflecting the
gritty optimism of the Chinese who overcame prejudice and
adversity to build a unique place for themselves in
North America.
1. Chinese Americans – Juvenile fiction. 2. Children's
stories, Canadian. [1. Chinese Americans – Fiction.
2. Short stories] I. Title.
PZ7.Y365Tal 1990 [Fic] 89-12643
ISBN 0-02-793621-X

Design by Michael Solomon
Set in Berthold Caslon Book by Canadian Composition
Printed and bound in Hong Kong by
Everbest Printing Co. Ltd.

To Vernon and Cecilia.

P.Y.

To my wife, Linda.

S.N.

Contents

Spirits of the Railway

Spirits of the Railway

ONE summer many, many years ago, heavy floodwaters suddenly swept through south China again. Farmer Chu and his family fled to high ground and wept as the rising river drowned their rice crops, their chickens and their water buffalo.

With their food and farm gone, Farmer Chu went to town to look for work. But a thousand other starving peasants were already there. So when he heard there was work across the ocean in the New World, he borrowed some money, bought a ticket, and off he sailed.

Long months passed as his family waited to hear from him. Farmer Chu's wife fell ill from worry and weariness. From her hard board bed she called out her husband's name over and over, until at last her eldest son borrowed money to cross the Pacific in search of his father.

For two months, young Chu listened to waves batter the groaning planks of the ship as it crossed the ocean. For two months he dreaded that he might drown at any minute. For two months he thought of nothing but his father and his family.

Finally he arrived in a busy port city. He asked everywhere for his father, but no one in Chinatown had heard the name. There were thousands of Chinese flung throughout the New World, he was told. Gold miners scrabbled along icy rivers, farmers ploughed the long low valleys, and laborers traveled through towns and forests, from job to job. Who could find one single man in this enormous wilderness?

Young Chu was soon penniless. But he was young and strong, and he feared neither danger nor hard labor. He joined a work gang of thirty Chinese, and a steamer ferried them up a river canyon to build the railway.

When the morning mist lifted, Chu's mouth fell open. On both sides of the rushing river, gray mountains rose like walls to block the sky. The rock face dropped into ragged cliffs that only eagles could ascend and jutted out from cracks where scrawny trees clung. Never before had he seen such towering ranges of dark raw rock.

The crew pitched their tents and began to work. They hacked at hills with hand-scoops and shovels to level a pathway for the train. Their hammers and chisels chipped boulders into gravel and fill. Their dynamite and drills thrust tunnels deep into the mountain. At night, the crew would sit around the campfire chewing tobacco, playing cards and talking.

From one camp to another, the men trekked up the rail line, their food and tools dangling from sturdy shoulder poles. When they met other workers, Chu would run ahead and shout his father's name and ask for news. But the workers just shook their heads grimly.

"Search no more, young man!" one grizzled old worker said. "Don't you know that too many have died here? My own brother was buried alive in a mudslide."

"My uncle was killed in a dynamite blast," muttered another. "No one warned him about the fuse."

The angry memories rose and swirled like smoke among the workers.

"The white boss treats us like mules and dogs!"

"They need a railway to tie this nation together, but they can't afford to pay decent wages."

"What kind of country is this?"

Chu listened, but still he felt certain that his father was alive.

Then winter came and halted all work. Snows buried everything under a heavy blanket of white. The white boss went to town to live in a warm hotel, but Chu and the workers stayed in camp. The men tied potato sacks around their feet and huddled by the fire, while ice storms howled like wolves through the mountains. Chu thought the winter would never end.

When spring finally arrived, the survivors struggled outside and shook the chill from their bones. They dug graves for two workers who had succumbed to sickness. They watched the river surge alive from the melting snow. Work resumed, and Chu began to search again for his father.

Late one afternoon, the gang reached a mountain with a half-finished tunnel. As usual, Chu ran up to shout his father's name, but before he could say a word, other workers came running out of the tunnel.

"It's haunted!" they cried. "Watch out! There are ghosts inside!"

"Dark figures slide soundlessly through the rocks!" one man whispered. "We hear heavy footsteps approaching but never arriving. We hear sighs and groans coming from corners where no man stands."

Chu's friends dropped their packs and refused to set up camp. But the white boss rode up on his horse and shook his fist at the men. "No work, no pay!" he shouted. "Now get to work!"

Then he galloped off. The workers squatted on the rocks and looked helplessly at one another. They needed the money badly for food and supplies.

Chu stood up. "What is there to fear?" he cried. "The ghosts have no reason to harm us. There is no reason to be afraid. We have hurt no one."

"Do you want to die?" a man called out.

"I will spend the night inside the tunnel," Chu declared as the men muttered unbelievingly. "Tomorrow we can work."

Chu took his bedroll, a lamp, and food and marched into the mountain. He heard the crunch of his boots and water dripping. He knelt to light his lamp. Rocks lay in loose piles everywhere, and the shadowy walls closed in on him.

At the end of the tunnel he sat down and ate his food. He closed his eyes and wondered where his father was. He pictured his mother weeping in her bed and heard her voice calling his father's name. He lay down, pulled his blankets close, and eventually he fell asleep.

Chu awoke gasping for breath. Something heavy was pressing down on his chest. He tried to raise his arms but could not. He clenched his fists and summoned all his strength, but still he was paralyzed. His eyes strained into the darkness, but saw nothing.

Suddenly the pressure eased and Chu groped for the lamp. As the chamber sprang into light, he cried, "What do you want? Who are you?"

Silence greeted him, and then a murmur sounded from behind. Chu spun around and saw a figure in the shadows. He slowly raised the lamp. The flickering light traveled up blood-stained trousers and a mud-encrusted jacket. Then Chu saw his father's face.

"Papa!" he whispered, lunging forward.

"No! Do not come closer!" The figure stopped him. "I am not of your world. Do not embrace me."

Tears rose in Chu's eyes. "So, it's true," he choked. "You … you have left us …"

His father's voice quivered with rage. "I am gone, but I am not done yet. My son, an accident here killed many men. A fuse exploded before the workers could run. A ton of rock dropped on us and crushed us flat. They buried the whites in a churchyard, but our bodies were thrown into the river, where the current swept us away. We have no final resting place."

Chu fell upon his knees. "What shall I do?"

His father's words filled the tunnel. "Take chopsticks; they shall be our bones. Take straw matting; that can be our flesh. Wrap them together and tie them tightly. Take the bundles to the mountain top high above the nests of eagles, and cover us with soil. Pour tea over our beds. Then we shall sleep in peace."

When Chu looked up, his father had vanished. He stumbled out of the tunnel and blurted the story to his friends. Immediately they prepared the bundles and sent him off with ropes and a shovel to the foot of the cliff, and Chu began to climb.

When he swung himself over the top of the cliff, he was so high up that he thought he could see the distant ocean. He dug the graves deeper than any wild animal could dig, and laid the bundles gently in the earth.

Then Chu brought his fists together above his head and bowed three times. He knelt and touched his forehead to the soil three times. In a loud clear voice he declared, "Three times I bow, three things I vow. Your pain shall stop now, your sleep shall soothe you now, and I will never forget you. Farewell."

Then, hanging onto the rope looped around a tree, Chu slid slowly back down the cliff. When he reached the bottom, he looked back and saw that the rope had turned into a giant snake that was sliding smoothly up the rock face.

"Good," he smiled to himself. "It will guard the graves well." Then he returned to the camp, where he and his fellow workers lit their lamps and headed into the tunnel. And spirits never again disturbed them, nor the long trains that came later.

Sons and Daughters

SONS AND DAUGHTERS

IF you had been in Chinatown in the early days, and if Merchant Moy had passed you on the thick wooden sidewalk, you would never have guessed that he was the richest Chinese in town. His face always wore a frown, even though his store and family name was carved into the largest wood scroll ever seen, painted with gleaming gold and hanging from the tallest building in Chinatown. Merchant Moy never spoke or joked, even when customers crowded around his counters from morning till midnight, peering into every rack and bin, into every stack and barrel.

No, Merchant Moy was not a happy man.

He was forty years old, and he had spent all his youth building his business. Still, he had one dream. More than anything in the world, he wanted a family. In particular, he wanted sons to carry on his family name. In China, the surname Moy was little known and linked only to poor peasants. Now Merchant Moy wanted everyone to know how rich his name and business had become.

Above his storefront, he had built spacious apartments large enough for many children and many more grandchildren. His wife was in China, and for a long time she was afraid to cross the ocean. So when she finally changed her mind and stepped off the steamship, there was no man happier than Merchant Moy.

Soon after her arrival, Madame Moy's belly swelled out broad and big, and Merchant Moy waited with bated breath. When the day came, he sat beside the bedroom door, and then he heard the loud wailings of a baby. The midwife hurried forth.

"Congratulations, sir!" she cried. "Twins have been born!"

"Twins?" Merchant Moy's heart skipped. "The gods are smiling to give me two babies at once!"

"Yes, sir," continued the midwife. "You have two healthy girls!"

"Girls?" Merchant Moy's heart sank. "How is my wife?" he asked.

The midwife shook her head sadly. "It was a difficult birth," she replied. "She lives, but she will never bear more babies."

Merchant Moy cursed. Without sons, the Moy family name would disappear. Without sons, he had no one to carry on his business. His entire life's work would be worthless.

Merchant Moy stood silent, thinking. Finally he spoke.

"Tell Chinatown that twin boys have been born," he ordered. "Tell Chinatown we will hold the biggest banquet ever seen. Tell Chinatown the gods have smiled on the Moy family today!" He told the midwife to register the birth of twin sons, and paid her well for her trouble. Then he went to his wife, who lay weak and weary in bed.

"My beloved," he said. "Let me take the children to China. My aged parents wish to see them, before it is too late. You rest here, and let the servants care for you."

Then Merchant Moy went down to the station. At one wicket he bought the steamship tickets. At another wicket he got the forms he would need when he returned from China. He filled out one form for himself, and then he filled out two for his children, putting in boy names for the babies. Then they all sailed for China.

Upon arriving, Merchant Moy summoned his servant to him. "Go out to the countryside," he ordered. "Find me a pair of baby boys and buy them for me. No price is too high."

The servant followed the dirt roads out to the fields and villages and went into the gray brick farmhouses to inquire among the peasants. Many had baby girls to sell, but even the hungriest fathers would try to keep a baby boy. Like Merchant Moy, they believed that only boys could keep the family name alive. And to them, after food and shelter, there was nothing as important as the family name.

But eventually the servant found a family long without food and shelter—a family who could not resist Merchant Moy's money.

When the servant returned to his master, a broad smile crossed Merchant Moy's face. Without a second thought, he gave away his own two daughters and packed his bags.

Merchant Moy sailed for home with his new sons. At the station, inspectors checked his papers closely, but they found that the babies were indeed twin boys as the documents showed.

When Madame Moy discovered what her husband had done, she wept and wept and would not eat. She sat like a statue. She felt as if someone had cut her open and cast a piece of her into the cold dark ocean.

Then she heard the boy babies crying, crying for milk, crying to be fed. Her face softened, and she went to them.

Madame Moy raised the two boys as if they were her own. She brushed their cheeks to hers, nursed them and purred to them. She showered them with love and attention.

As the years went by, the two boys grew up bright and healthy. They worked hard at school and studied Chinese. On weekends they worked with the warehouse men and in their father's office, where they balanced the ledger books. Merchant Moy and his wife smiled softly, for they were very proud of their sons.

When the boys turned eighteen, Merchant Moy sent them to China to look for wives, for there were few unmarried women in Chinatown. When the boys returned, a pair of twin sisters came with them. Madame Moy liked the girls immediately, for they were high-spirited, quick to laugh, and quick to learn. When the young people were married, all of Chinatown came to the gala banquet, with money and red-wrapped gifts to wish the Moy family well.

The sons and their wives moved into the family quarters above the store. A year passed, and Merchant Moy sat back to wait for grandchildren. Another year passed, but still there were no babies. Merchant Moy began to fret and frown again. He made sure the girls ate plenty of hot soup with life-giving seeds and herbs. Still, no new generation showed its head.

Merchant Moy sent his sons and their wives to the herbalist, the doctor who used wild herbs, preserved roots and dried animal parts to heal people according to ancient prescriptions. The wise old man listened carefully to their pulses and peered into their eyes, but he pronounced them all in perfect health.

Then Merchant Moy sent them to the western doctor at the city hospital. The efficient young man used his thermometer to take their temperatures while he poked and prodded high and low. He pronounced them all in perfect health.

Merchant Moy worried more and more. "Soon I will die," he thought. "I must have grandchildren!"

Finally he went to pray at the temple. He thrust two thick candles and three sticks of incense into the big brass urn. He offered wine to the gods above, and then he knelt before the altar and asked for answers.

The temple-keeper spoke. "The gods above, they say, no man can wed his sister."

Merchant Moy's face paled. Could it be? Could his sons have married the daughters he had discarded two decades earlier?

"But they are not true brothers and sisters," he prayed. "They come from different parents!"

"The gods say, they have the same name!" said the temple-keeper.

Merchant Moy bowed his head. "What can I do? My daughters were born with my name, but lost it when I gave them away. As for my boys, I gave them the Moy name. If I take it away now, the family name will be lost forever!"

But the gods would say no more.

As Merchant Moy left the temple, he knew that he alone had placed this curse on his children. In the following weeks his hair turned a snowy white. His head sagged from dread and his shoulders stooped. When he looked at his sons and daughters, he wanted to weep, but he could not.

Not long after, Merchant Moy died. When his will was read, everyone was puzzled. He had instructed that all his business and buildings and bank accounts be evenly divided between his two sons. But one strange condition was attached. His sons must give notice and change their family name!

The sons were mystified, but they obeyed the instructions. And so the Moy name was lost to the store, lost to the memory of the business that Merchant Moy had built. Only Madame Moy suspected why her husband had done this. She wept silently and drew her children close to her, but she told them nothing, for she wanted them to remember their father with love.

Soon the daughters gave birth—one boy, one girl. Madame Moy was overjoyed. She smiled and prayed for her husband's spirit to rest peacefully now. The name was lost, but the family would live on.

THE FRIENDS OF KWAN MING

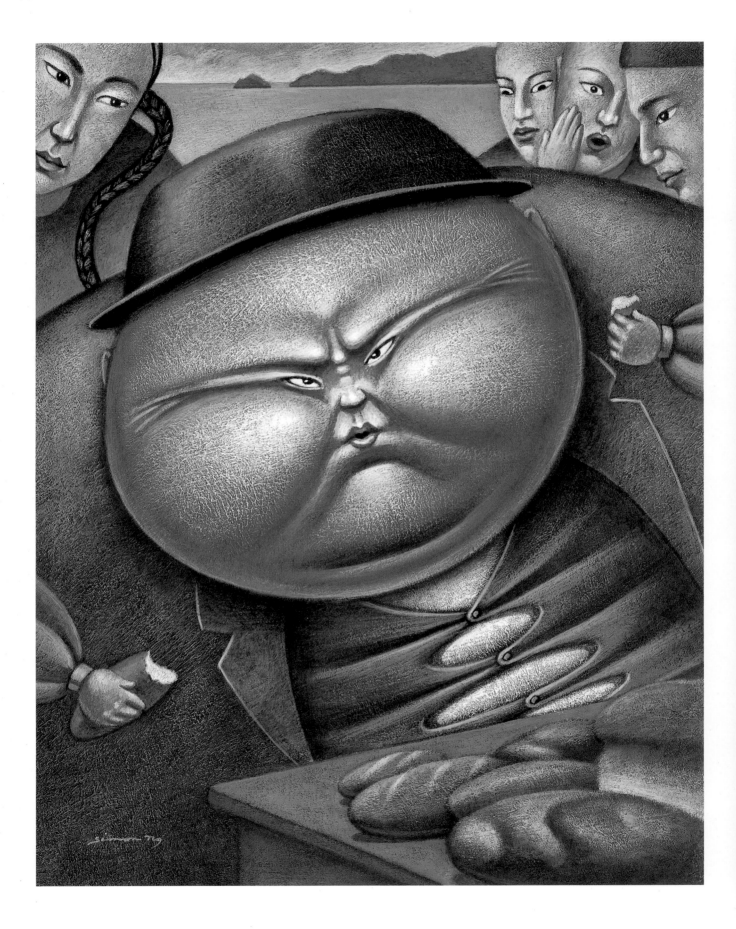

THE FRIENDS OF KWAN MING

WHEN his father died, the peasant Kwan Ming was forced to sell his little plot of paddy and the old family house to pay for the burial. After the funeral, Kwan Ming looked around at the banana trees surrounding his village, and saw that he had nothing left to his name —not even one chipped roof tile. He had just enough money to buy a steamship ticket to the New World, where he had heard jobs were plentiful.

"I can start a new life there," he told his mother. "I will send money home."

The voyage lasted six weeks, over rocky waves and through screaming storms. Kwan Ming huddled together with hundreds of other Chinese deep in the ship's hold. There he became fast friends with Chew Lap, Tam Yim and Wong Foon—men from neighboring villages. If one friend took sick, the others fetched him food and water. If one friend had bad luck gambling, the others lent him money to recover his losses. Together the three men ate, told jokes, and shared their dreams for the future.

When they arrived in the New World, everyone scattered throughout the port city to search for work. Kwan Ming hurried to the warehouse district, to the train station, and to the waterfront, but doors slammed in his face because he was Chinese. So he went to every store and laundry in Chinatown, and to every farm outside town. But there was not a job to be found anywhere, for there were too many men looking for work in a country that was still too young.

Every night Kwan Ming trudged back to the inn where he was staying with his three friends. Like him, they, too, had been searching for work but had found nothing. Every night, as they ate their meager meal of rice dotted with soya sauce, the friends shared information about the places they had visited and the people they had met. And every night Kwan Ming worried more and more about his mother, and how she was faring.

"If I don't find work soon, I'm going back to China," Chew Lap declared one evening.

"What for, fool?" asked Tam Yim. "Things are worse there!"

"But at least I will be with my family!" retorted Chew Lap.

"Your family needs money for food more than they need your company," Wong Foon commented. "Don't forget that."

Then a knock was heard at the door, and the innkeeper pushed his way into the tiny attic room.

"Good news!" he cried out. "I have found a job for each of you!"

The men leapt eagerly to their feet.

"Three of the jobs are well-paying and decent," announced the innkeeper. "But the fourth job is, well . . ." He coughed sadly.

For the first time since they had met, the four men eyed one another warily, like four hungry cats about to pounce on a bird.

"The biggest bakery in Chinatown needs a worker," said the innkeeper. "You'll always be warm next to the oven. Who will go?"

"You go, Chew Lap," Kwan Ming said firmly. "Your parents are ill and need money for medicine."

"The finest tailor in Chinatown wants an apprentice," continued the innkeeper. "The man who takes this job will be able to throw away those thin rags you wear."

"That's for you, Tam Yim," declared Kwan Ming. "You have

four little ones waiting for food in China."

"The best shoemaker in Chinatown needs an assistant," said the innkeeper. "He pays good wages. Who wants to cut leather and stitch boots?"

"You go, Wong Foon," Kwan Ming stated. "You said the roof of your house in China needs repair. Better get new tiles before the rainy season starts."

"The last job is for a houseboy." The innkeeper shook his head. "The pay is low. The boss owns the biggest mansion in town, but he is also the stingiest man around!"

Kwan Ming had no choice but to take this job, for he knew his mother would be desperate for money. So off he went.

The boss was fatter than a cast-iron stove and as cruel as a blizzard at midnight. Kwan Ming's room was next to the furnace, so black soot and coal dust covered his pillow and blankets. It was difficult to save money, and the servants had to fight over the leftovers for their meals.

Every day Kwan Ming swept and washed every floor in the mansion. He moved the heavy oak tables and rolled up the carpets. The house was so big, that when Kwan Ming finally finished cleaning the last room, the first one was dirty all over again.

One afternoon Kwan Ming was mopping the front porch when his boss came running out. In his hurry, he slipped and crashed down the stairs. Kwan Ming ran over to help, but the fat man turned on him.

"You turtle!" he screamed as his neck purpled and swelled. "You lazy oaf! You doorknob! You rock-brain! You're fired!"

Kwan Ming stood silently for a long moment. Then he spoke. "Please, sir, give me another chance. I will work even harder if you let me stay."

The boss listened and his eyes narrowed. Then he coughed

loudly. "Very well, Kwan Ming, I won't fire you," he said. "But I will have to punish you, for you have ruined this suit and scuffed my boots and made me miss my dinner."

Kwan Ming nodded miserably.

"Then find me the following things in three days' time!" the boss ordered. "Bring me a fine woolen suit that will never tear. Bring me a pair of leather boots that will never wear out. And bring me forty loaves of bread that will never go stale. Otherwise you are finished here, and I will see that you never find another job!"

Kwan Ming shuddered as he ran off. The old man's demands sounded impossible. Where would he find such items?

In despair, Kwan Ming wandered through the crowded streets of Chinatown. He sat on the raised wooden sidewalk because he had nowhere else to go.

Suddenly, familiar voices surrounded him.

"Kwan Ming, where have you been?"

"Kwan Ming, how is your job?"

"Kwan Ming, why do you never visit us?"

Kwan Ming looked up and saw his three friends smiling down at him. They pulled him up and pulled him off to the teahouse, where they ate and drank. When Kwan Ming told his friends about his predicament, the men clapped him on the shoulder.

"Don't worry!" exclaimed Tam Yim. "I'll make the woolen suit you need."

"I'll make the boots," added Wong Foon.

"And I'll make the bread," exclaimed Chew Lap.

Three days later, Kwan Ming's friends delivered the goods they had promised. An elegant suit of wool hung over a gleaming pair of leather boots, and forty loaves of fresh-baked bread were lined up in neat rows on the dining-room table.

Kwan Ming's boss waddled into the room and his eyes lit up.

He put on the suit, and his eyebrows arched in surprise at how well it fit. Then he sat down and tried on the boots, which slid onto his feet as if they had been buttered.

Then the boss sliced into the bread and started eating. The bread was so soft, so sweet, and so moist that he couldn't stop. Faster and faster he chewed. He ate twelve loaves, then thirteen, then twenty.

The boss's stomach swelled like a circus tent, and his feet bloated out like balloons. But the well-sewn suit and sturdy boots held him tight like a gigantic sausage. The man shouted for help. He tried to stand up, but he couldn't even get out of his chair. He kicked his feet about like a baby throwing a tantrum.

But before anyone could do a thing, there was a shattering *Bang!*

Kwan Ming stared at the chair and blinked his eyes in astonishment. For there was nothing left of his boss.

He had exploded into a million little pieces.

GINGER FOR THE HEART

Ginger for the Heart

The buildings of Chinatown are stoutly constructed of brick, and while some are broad and others thin, they rise no higher than four solid storeys. Many contain stained-glass windows decorated with flower and diamond patterns, and others boast balconies with fancy wrought-iron railings.

Only one building stands above the rest. Its turret-like tower is visible even from the harbor, because the cone-shaped roof is made of copper.

In the early days, Chang the merchant tailor owned this building. He used the main floor for his store and rented out the others. But he kept the tower room for his own use, for the sun filled it with light. This was the room where his wife and daughter worked.

His daughter's name was Yenna, and her beauty was beyond compare. She had ivory skin, sparkling eyes, and her hair hung long and silken, shining like polished ebony. All day long she and her mother sat by the tower window and sewed with silver needles and silken threads. They sang songs while they worked, and their voices rose in wondrous harmonies.

In all Chinatown, the craftsmanship of Yenna and her mother was considered the finest. Search as they might, customers could not discern where holes had once pierced their shirts. Buttonholes never stretched out of shape, and seams were all but invisible.

One day, a young man came into the store laden with garments for mending. His shoulders were broad and strong, yet his eyes were soft and caring. Many times he came, and many times he saw Yenna. For hours he would sit and watch her work. They fell deeply in love, though few words were spoken between them.

Spring came and boats bound for the northern gold fields began to sail again. It was time for the young man to go. He had borrowed money to pay his way over to the New World, and now he had to repay his debts. Onto his back he threw his blankets and tools, food and warm jackets. Then he set off with miners from around the world, clutching gold pans and shovels.

Yenna had little to give him in farewell. All she found in the kitchen was a ginger root as large as her hand. As she stroked its brown knobs and bumpy eyes, she whispered to him, "This will warm you in the cold weather. I will wait for you, but, like this piece of ginger, I, too, will age and grow dry." Then she pressed her lips to the ginger, and turned away.

"I will come back," the young man said. "The fire burning for you in my heart can never be extinguished."

Thereafter, Yenna lit a lamp at every nightfall and set it in the tower window. Rains lashed against the glass, snow piled low along the ledge, and ocean winds rattled the frame. But the flame did not waver, even though the young man never sent letters. Yenna did not weep uselessly, but continued to sew and sing with her mother.

There were few unmarried women in Chinatown, and many men came to seek Yenna's hand in marriage. Rich gold miners and sons of successful merchants bowed before her, but she always looked away. They gave her grand gifts, but still she shook her head, until finally the men grew weary and called her crazy. In China, parents arranged all marriages, and daughters became the property of their husbands. But Chang the merchant tailor treasured his daughter's happiness and let her be.

One winter, an epidemic ravaged the city. When it was over,

Chang had lost his wife and his eyesight. Yenna led him up to the tower where he could feel the sun and drifting clouds move across his face. She began to sew again, and while she sewed, she sang for her father. The lamp continued to burn steadily at the tower window as she worked. With twice the amount of work to do, she labored long after dusk. She fed the flame more oil and sent her needle skimming through the heavy fabrics. Nimbly her fingers braided shiny cords and coiled them into butterfly buttons. And when the wick sputtered into light each evening, Yenna's heart soared momentarily into her love's memories. Nights passed into weeks, months turned into years, and four years quickly flew by.

One day a dusty traveler came into the store and flung a bundle of ragged clothes onto the counter. Yenna shook out the first shirt, and out rolled a ginger root. Taking it into her hand, she saw that pieces had been nibbled off, but the core of the root was still firm and fragrant.

She looked up. There stood the man she had promised to wait for. His eyes appeared older and wiser.

"Your gift saved my life several times," he said. "The fire of the ginger is powerful indeed."

"Why is the ginger root still firm and heavy?" she wondered. "Should it not have dried and withered?"

"I kept it close to my heart and my sweat coated it. In lonely moments, my tears soaked it." His calloused hands reached out for her. "Your face has not changed."

"Nor has my heart," she replied. "I have kept a lamp burning all these years."

"So I have heard," he smiled. "Will you come away with me now? It has taken many years to gather enough gold to buy a farm. I have built you a house on my land."

For the first time since his departure, tears cascaded down Yenna's face. She shook her head. "I cannot leave. My father needs me."

"Please come with me," the young man pleaded. "You will be very happy, I promise."

Yenna swept the wetness from her cheeks. "Stay with me and work this store instead," she implored.

The young man stiffened and stated proudly, "A man does not live in his wife's house." And the eyes that she remembered so well gleamed with determination.

"But this is a new land," she cried. "Must we forever follow the old ways?"

She reached out for him, but he brushed her away. With a curse, he hurled the ginger root into the fireplace. As the flames leapt up, Yenna's eyes blurred. The young man clenched and unclenched his fists in anger. They stood like stone.

At last the man turned to leave, but suddenly he knelt at the fireplace. Yenna saw him reach in with the tongs and pull something out of the flames.

"Look!" he whispered in amazement. "The ginger refuses to be burnt! The flames cannot touch it!"

Yenna looked and saw black burn marks charring the root, but when she took it in her hand, she found it still firm and moist. She held it to her nose, and found the fragrant sharpness still there.

The couple embraced and swore to stay together. They were married at a lavish banquet attended by all of Chinatown. There, the father passed his fingers over his son-in-law's face and nodded in satisfaction.

Shortly after, the merchant Chang died, and the young couple moved away. Yenna sold the business and locked up the tower room. But on nights when boats pull in from far away, they say a flicker of light can still be seen in that high window. And Chinese women are reminded that ginger is one of their best friends.

GAMBLER'S EYES

Gambler's Eyes

In the New World, in any town with a Chinatown, there would always be a gambling hall. Usually it was a log cabin perched at the edge of the forest. There the miners and loggers and farmers would gather, crowding around heavy plank tables. The fireplace and gas lamps threw out smoke and a dim yellow glow that swirled and mixed with the thick shouts and laughter of men. Deep into the night they played, fishing for new fortunes as they threw out their savings as bait.

One night, the door to one such place swung open. Silence fell like a heavy blanket over the room. The jingle of coins ceased, the grunts of drunken men shushed, and everyone turned to stare.

A man stood in the doorway. He was tall and thin, with a face darkened by the sun and hardened by the wind. His jacket was ragged and patched, and a knotted cloth bundle was slung across his back.

The stranger stood for a moment to get his bearings. His eyes were long sealed with hardened spittle and settled dust.

Never before had a blind man come into the gambling hall.

"Hey, brother," called out one fellow. "You're in the wrong place. Don't you know this is a game hall?"

The blind man's cane whipped from side to side as he strode to the fan-tan table, and the bystanders fell aside.

Then the blind man threw a thick roll of bills onto the table.

"This money, is it not good here?" he asked.

The dealer smiled. "Easy earnings tonight!" he muttered to himself. Then he beckoned to everyone. "Come, come, let's play!" He threw a handful of game coins onto the table and covered them with a brass cup. "Lay your bets!" he shouted.

The blind man hesitated.

"Come, come, come," the dealer cried, shaking the cup and rattling the coins. "Let's play, let's play!"

The blind man stood without moving. Finally he peeled off four large bills and thrust them on the three slot.

"No other bets?" called the dealer.

The crowd coughed and shifted. Two idlers who gambled every night snickered aloud.

"You don't want to toy with the blind," said one. "They can't see, and they'll call you a cheat if they lose!"

"Blind men are bad luck," called out the other. "Who needs that in a place like this?"

The dealer ignored the unfriendly rumble and went on. "Let's open!" he cried. He lifted the cup and sorted the coins into groups of four. "Four, eight, twelve, sixteen, twenty . . ." and so he counted. When he got to the tail end, lo and behold, three coins were left! The blind man had won!

"Play again?" asked the dealer. He threw another handful of coins under the brass cup and shook them.

The blind man nodded. He slid ten big bills on the two slot, and then the dealer uncovered the coins to count. And when he got to the tail end, lo and behold, two coins were left! The blind man had won again!

The blind man played another three rounds, betting more and more each time. And time after time, he was the winner.

The crowd muttered in amazement at his luck. The dealer tightened his thin lips and waited grimly. He had seen this before. A man might win a few rounds, but sooner or later, all the money bounced back to the dealer's side of the board.

Now the spectators reached into their pockets. The blind man listened to the dealer's impatient jingling and finally set a bet on the three slot. Right away, everyone in the room added their cash to his. A mountain of money faced the dealer.

The dealer sighed and started to count the game coins. When he reached the end, lo and behold, only one coin was left! The dealer smiled a smile that stretched from ear to ear. The groans of forty men hit the roof as their money was swept away.

"Play again?" asked the dealer eagerly.

The blind man shook his head. "My luck is finished," he declared. Then he turned from the table and groped his way to the door.

The two gamblers who had snickered aloud earlier spat out their tobacco in anger. They had lost all their cash with the blind man's bet. Without a word, they went out after him. One seized an iron bar, the other a length of wood. They crept up as quiet as could be, and then they struck. But the blind man ducked and jumped aside. His cane swung and knocked out one man. As the other man hit out again, the blind man hopped nimbly away.

The second man winced. How could a blind man fight so well? He readied his iron bar again, and the two men faced each other, their steps tracing a circle in the dust.

"You think you're smart, don't you?" growled the gambler. "You cheated us all!"

"You tricked yourselves," retorted the blind man calmly. "Are you sure you want to fight me?"

The gambler looked up with a snarl. As he swung his bar, the blind man's eyes flashed open. They glinted blue-green, sharp as mountain ice, hard as emeralds.

The gambler screamed and ran.

Weeks later, the blind man was seen in a distant town, and then in another. It was always the same. He won his wagers and then he left when greedy gamblers tried to wager with him.

Late one day, the blind man came to a new place, to a new game hall. He made his way to the table and laid down a wager, but the dealer stopped him.

"Don't bother," he ordered. "We know your game, blind man. You can't play here, nor in any town near or far in this territory. You are finished, do you understand?"

The blind man stumbled back and down he sat with a heavy sigh. When he opened his mouth, the men moved warily away.

"All of you," he said, "you wonder where I come from, why I win so well. Is that not so? I will tell you now, since I can gamble no more. You see, my father came from China to seek his fortune here, but my mother was white, and she gave me these."

He opened his eyes and everyone saw the blue-green flashes – blue as sky, green as pine.

"When I was a child," he continued, "I could go nowhere with eyes like these. Storekeepers turned away. Children danced circles around me. Whites and Chinese alike, they mocked my mixed blood. So I shut my eyes and I opened my ears. As long as no one saw my eyes, they let me by. Now I hear what you cannot hear: the hearts of greedy gamblers, the pulse of petty thieves. I hear the game coins rattle under the brass cup, and the unique sound that each combination makes. I hear everything."

With that, the blind man rose and threw down his cane. He walked out the door and into the dark, and was never seen again.

Forbidden Fruit

Forbidden Fruit

Many years ago, in a valley deep in the heart of the New World, the farmer, Fong, cleared the forest and staked out his land. Day after day he pushed a wooden plough through the unbroken soil and drew long dark lines to the hazy horizon.

Through the long hot summers Farmer Fong watered his crops; through the deep dark winters he built up his barn. Working the soil nourished his soul just as the food he grew nourished his body. How he smiled when the sunshine soaked his back, or when rain filled the furrows in his field.

Farmer Fong smiled also at the thought of his three sons and one daughter. Their mother had died giving birth to the baby sister, but she was loved the best. The three boys made sure that her farm chores were never too heavy, and they helped her in the kitchen. Farmer Fong watched his children grow into fine adults, and he dreamed of how his farm would expand and prosper.

But the three boys did not stay. Their ears perked to the tales of travelers, and their eyes followed horses headed for far-off places. Farmer Fong tried to make them see the magic of the soil that moved him, but the words did not come easily. One by one the sons went off. The eldest son strapped on a shoulder pack and panned for gold along the northern rivers. The second son seized a shovel and stoked coal inside steamships sailing along the rocky coast. The youngest hitched his saddle and worked on the wagon trains and stagecoaches.

Farmer Fong watched bitterly as his sons trekked away. He shouted after them, "If you leave now, you are no longer my sons! Never cross my gate again, never call me Father! You are all finished!"

He turned and hurled his fury at the daughter. He worked her in the fields like an ox, and he complained about her cooking at every meal. He stamped his boot on the floorboards to waken her in the mornings and cursed her mother for bearing such wayward boys. But the daughter understood his anger and let it flow by her.

One day a young man appeared at their door. He was covered with dust. "I have walked many miles looking for work," he said. "I will work for you if you can give me shelter and three meals a day."

Farmer Fong looked the man over and nodded. The young man's hair was cropped short and bristled thick and full. Sweat and blowing dust had hardened his shirt and pants.

The daughter smiled at the man and rejoiced that someone had come to share her labor.

Through the long hot summer the daughter and the young man worked side by side. Together they pulled at weeds and pumped for water. They pedaled the waterwheel and made crates and sacks for packing. At harvest time, they spent weary weeks bent over the fields, hacking and pulling at the crops. They labored as equals and darkened under the sun.

And every evening after dinner, they sat on the verandah, rubbing their aching muscles and fanning themselves. The daughter wept softly, remembering her brothers, and the man held her in his arms. But nothing could be done.

One morning after the harvest, the farmhand put on a clean shirt and asked Farmer Fong if he could marry his daughter. Farmer Fong refused, saying his daughter could not marry a man without means. Without a word, the young man gathered his goods and departed. The daughter watched him leave just as her brothers had done before, and she felt a thin bolt of lightning lance her heart.

She crumpled onto the floor and was carried to bed where she lay with her eyes closed, scarcely breathing. Farmer Fong watched helplessly as his beloved daughter grew weaker, and his anger melted. He sent for ancient herbs, he sent for the doctor. But even the strongest medicines and richest broths could not restore her strength.

The doctor shook his head. "I can do nothing," he said. "It is not a sickness of the body."

Farmer Fong knelt by the bed and grasped his daughter's hand. "Tell me what makes you ill, daughter!" he cried. "Tell me what will set you well again!"

Her eyelids lifted and she whispered, "Bring me news of the one I love."

Farmer Fong swallowed hard. Then he sent urgent letters to his three sons. He told them of their sister's illness and described the farmhand. He ordered them to find him. "Please hurry!" he wrote.

Weeks passed. Then one day the eldest son strode in from the mountains. "Your loved one pans for gold by an icy stream," he reported. "He sends these tokens of his love."

He placed cool lumps of gold and jade into his sister's hands. But they fell from her fingers, because she knew her brother was lying.

Then the second brother came back from the ocean. "He has set up shop as a merchant in a port city," he told her. "He sends these gifts to speak his heart."

He unrolled bolts of soft silk and shiny brocade before her, but she knew his story was false, too.

Finally the youngest son galloped up on his horse. "He is fighting heaven and earth to reclaim new farmlands!" he cried. "He had nothing but these to send you."

He pressed some dry, wrinkled seeds into her hands. They softened at her touch and tiny tendrils began to sprout. The daughter felt life tingle warm inside her like the first sunshine of spring. Swiftly she set the seeds into pots by her window and watched them grow.

When the days grew mild enough, she planted the seedlings in the soil outside. Daily she tended the rows, feeding and speaking to the plants as if they were human. Farmer Fong smiled with relief as his daughter's health improved.

Then one night a cold spell seized the valley. The daughter rushed out to wrap cloth around her plants to keep the frost away, and Farmer Fong built a huge bonfire to warm the seedlings. But icy winds swept the fire out and blew the heat away. The little plants froze and shriveled. The daughter fell to the ground weeping and, in the arms of her sorrowing father, she soon died.

After she was buried, Farmer Fong found a small pot of seeds left in his daughter's room. He planted these with great care. When the seedlings came up, he propped panes of glass around them to protect them from the cold.

The plants sprang up tall and strong. Fruit appeared on the branches and slowly ripened into a deep blood-red. And when Farmer Fong bit into the fruit, the juices gushed sharp and sweet, reminding him of his daughter's gentle nature and his own foolish pride.

From then on, Farmer Fong continued to grow the plants. He built walls and ceilings of glass to enclose the long rows of seedlings. In these greenhouses, the tomatoes flourished and were shipped to all parts of the country. The brother on the wagon trail heaved crates of them. The sailor brother delivered them to far-flung coastal towns, and the miner found them on his plate when he came to town for a meal. They sniffed at the fruit's fragrance, stared at its glossy red and hefted its soft firmness in their dark strong hands. Thus they were always reminded of their sister and her love for the farmhand Johnson.

Rider Chan and the Night River

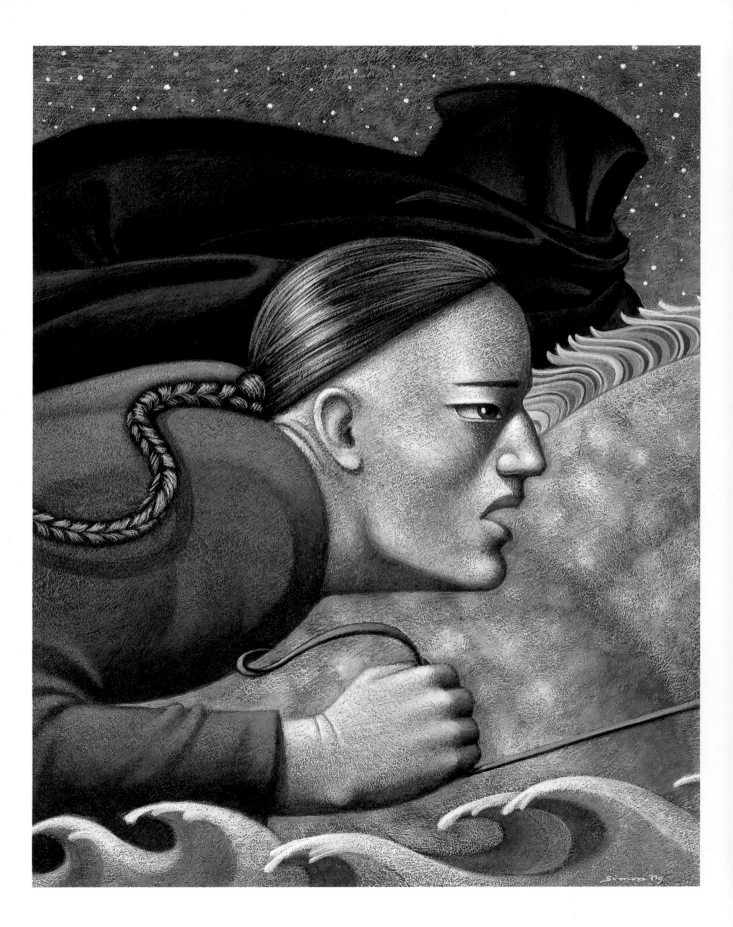

RIDER CHAN AND THE NIGHT RIVER

ONCE upon a time, two brothers were born in a small village near the ocean in south China. Their father died soon after, and it was their mother who raised them. Though she loved her sons deeply, she had little time for them, because she was kept very busy planting and harvesting rice, weaving cloth and mending clothes, and tending the pigs and chickens.

The two boys grew up, but they were as different as day from night. One brother helped his mother in the fields; the other played games with the lazy village children. One brother filled his mother's bowl with rice every night. The other ate and ran off without a word. One brother went deep into the hills to collect firewood, but the other feared the dark and refused to go.

When news of the gold rush in the New World reached the village, the mother decided that her sons should go there to seek their fortunes. Before they left, she bade them farewell and said, "You are grown men now, but still you must take care. The spirits in the New World are mighty and mysterious because there are fewer humans about. So beware!"

When the brothers reached the New World, the hard-working brother found work immediately. He became a courier because he was strong and husky, honest and fearless. It was his job to visit all the mining claims, all the shanty towns, and all the riverside camps throughout the gold country. He took messages and medicine to the miners and collected their letters and gold to be sent home to China. The miners called him Rider Chan and shouted out hearty welcomes whenever he galloped through on his swift gray horse.

Rider took care to send money back to his mother whenever he could. As for his brother, he disappeared into the gold territory like so many other miners, and Rider never heard from him again.

Late one afternoon, Rider Chan was asked to take some medicine to a miner who had been crushed under a rockslide. Rider did not usually travel at night, because outlaws knew that he carried gold and money, and they were always looking for opportunities to rob him. But a man's life was at stake, so Rider saddled up his horse, strapped on his pistol, and off he rode.

The moon shone full and bright that night. Rider Chan rode and rode, listening hard and staying well in the middle of the trail away from the shadows of the forest. Then he found his path cut off by a river—a river that glistened and shimmered as if it were alive.

Rider hesitated. He had heard tales that at night, the spirits of the drowned reached up from the bottom of lakes and rivers and pulled down new victims to replace their own rotted bodies.

He looked over the river. It seemed shallow and clear. He nudged his horse forward. The water crept up, past his toes and then to the top of his boots. Then, just as he spurred his horse to go faster, something grabbed his ankle.

"Go!" he screamed at his horse, but the hand under the water held him tight. His mount reared up and whinnied in panic, but could not move an inch.

Rider Chan drew his pistol and fired blindly into the water, but still his foot was held tight.

Beads of sweat broke out on his forehead. He dropped his gun and pulled at his leg with both his hands, but the water spirit was stronger. The horseman almost toppled into the river, but he caught himself. If he fell in, he knew he would be finished.

The spirit pulled harder and harder. Rider Chan began to weaken. He felt himself sliding off his horse.

"No!" he cried. "Don't take me! I have a mother to care for!"

But the dark spirit was not listening.

"Spare me!" Rider Chan pleaded. "I'm the courier! I carry medicine to a sick man!"

At once the grip loosened. Rider Chan galloped away. Safely ashore, he pinched his leg and discovered with a whoop of joy that he was still whole.

Then he turned back to the dark river. "Thank you for sparing my life," he called out. "I owe you a favor."

And at that, a figure suddenly rose out of the water. As it came close, Rider Chan saw slimy rags hanging from a body of bones. The stench of rotting flesh filled the night. Rider wanted to run, but he could not. After all, a promise was a promise.

The ghost drew near. "You are the courier," said a hollow voice. "I ask a simple favor. Bury my body on the shore. Wait, and when only my bones are left, dig them up and send them back to China."

The horseman bowed in agreement. He kept his eyes down, for he was afraid to see what the spirit's face might look like. But as the ghost passed by, heading for the shore, Rider Chan saw a knife protruding from its back.

"Who did this to you?" he cried out.

The ghost stopped. "I am ashamed to tell you," it said.

"Should not justice be done?" Rider Chan called out.

"I do not deserve justice," replied the ghost. "My partner and I struck gold, not far from here. I went to town to register the claim. Greed filled me, so I poisoned the food I took back. But my partner was greedy, too, and he jumped me and killed me. After dumping my body into the river, he ate the food I had brought. So he died, too."

Rider Chan shook his head. "May you both rest in peace."

"The tale is not finished," said the dark shadow. "My partner was your brother!"

Rider Chan stopped breathing.

"When you said you were the courier," continued the ghost, "I knew who you were. I want to make amends."

Rider Chan trembled.

"Our lucky find of gold is still safe, not far from here. Go there, gather up the gold, and send it back to your mother. Let our sad escapade bring some happiness to her. Alas, cougars and vultures have destroyed your brother's body, so no bones are left."

The courier thought it over. "I will send gold home to China. But I will let your story die here, between you and me, because the truth about my brother would surely kill my mother."

"So be it," said the ghost. And, after explaining where the gold lay, it fell down at Rider Chan's feet.

Rider Chan dug a grave by the river and covered the ghost's remains with soil and a few prayers. Following the ghost's instructions, he went upriver, gathered up the gold, and sent it back to his mother in China.

Not long after, she died, too, but with a peaceful smile on her face.

THE REVENGE OF THE IRON CHINK

The Revenge of the Iron Chink

In the old days, all up and down the west coast of the New World, at the mouths of mighty rivers, scores of fish canneries, bigger than barns, sat perched over the water. When the tide went out, the canneries looked like huge caterpillars—long rusty roofs of corrugated tin covered plank board bodies that stretched over hundreds of stilt-like legs. The smell of salt and fish was everywhere, and the shrill caws of seagulls filled the air.

The canneries stayed empty during the winter, but in the spring, crews of Chinese workers would arrive. They would throw open the creaky doors, brush away the cobwebs and start making thousands of tin cans. When the morning sun cut through the windows and lit the wall of waiting cans, the light would be as blinding as a curtain of diamonds.

Come summer, fishermen would sail forth and fling dark nets out to take the salmon from the sea. Back at the cannery, the Chinese would clean the fish and fill the cans with meat. The cans would be cooked and then shipped off to faraway markets.

Lee Jim was a boss in one such cannery. He had a crew of workers and, because he spoke English, he could translate the owner's orders to the men. When a boatload of fish came in, he could guess the exact number of cans that they would need with just one quick glance. Lee Jim watched that the fresh fish stayed cool and checked that nothing was wasted. When the butchers' knives got dull, he would sharpen them. So, even though Lee Jim was a boss, all the workers respected him.

At the cookhouse, though, Lee Jim ate alone. His workers crowded around tables and played card games late into the night. Lee Jim longed to laugh and joke with them, but he could not. Company rules said that boss men could not mix with the workers.

Every spring, Lee Jim brought his same old crew to the cannery. They knew the work so well that the owner didn't have to watch them. He was a fat little man who wore a tall hat and puffed on cigars. The workers called him Chimney Head. He would walk through the cannery and never look at the men, as if the smell of fish bothered him. He was always hidden inside his office, adding columns of numbers and counting his money.

Then Chimney Head began to change things in the cannery. To speed up the assembly line, he installed conveyor belts. To make the tin cans more quickly, he brought in a machine that whirred and clicked like a clock. Another machine jammed meat into cans as fast as fifty hands. Every year, some new improvement would be introduced.

Lee Jim's workers muttered nervously. They were working as hard as they could, yet Chimney Head was not happy. And each year, the crew became a little bit smaller because the machines took the men's places.

One busy morning, a brand-new machine was rolled onto the cannery floor. The machine was called the Iron Chink. Great clanking gears and sharp shiny blades spun and flashed in it. It was taller than any man and weighed over two tons. The Iron Chink could go all day and all night without stopping. It did the work of thirty trained butchers.

Chimney Head rubbed his fat hands in great excitement. Now he could can fish faster and more cheaply than ever before. And he was especially happy because he had been invited to send a case of fish to the Queen of England. The gift would display the province's fine salmon, as well as the high quality of the Iron Chink's work. Finally Chimney Head would be known as the fastest canner on the west coast.

Chimney Head stood up on a box and cleared his throat noisily. "I don't need you anymore," he announced to the workers. "Next year I can hire one or two men to run the Iron Chink, and it will do all the work. After tomorrow you can all pack your bags and leave on the next steamer. And you, Lee Jim, you can go, too. I don't need you anymore, either."

That night, the cookhouse was very quiet. The men wondered where they would find jobs. How would their families eat? "If only there was something we could do," they muttered.

Lee Jim sat with them, feeling angry and cheated. Hadn't he worked for Chimney Head for over twenty years? Hadn't he saved the cannery both time and money by being extra careful? And had he ever been sick on the job? No!

The next day, the final load of salmon arrived. The workers watched as the Iron Chink gobbled up the fish. The belts whirred, the wheels turned, and the gears zipped as smooth as ocean waves sliding over the sandy beach. The fish flew by and the tin cans were sealed like magic. Lee Jim scurried about as usual to make sure that everything ran smoothly. Finally, the cases were stacked up, and Chimney Head passed out the last pay envelopes.

The steamer sounded its whistle at the dock, and the workers ran to board the ship. Lee Jim was the last to leave.

As Chimney Head came by, Lee Jim held up his hands. Chimney Head saw that they were wrapped in bloody bandages.

"What happened to you, Lee Jim?" he cried.

Lee Jim stood up straight and tall. "I wanted to send a gift to the Queen, too. In two of the tins, she will find my baby fingers! I think she will find them as sweet as any salmon meat we have canned!"

The workers on the ship laughed and cheered from the railing. And before Chimney Head could say anything, Lee Jim had turned and jumped onto the boat.

Chimney Head sputtered in anger. He cursed and stamped his feet and threw his hat into the water, but there was nothing he could do.

As the steamer chugged away, the workers threw their arms around Lee Jim. They punched him playfully and told him, "You showed Chimney Head a thing or two! You're a brave man! Welcome to the working life, Lee Jim!"

Lee Jim looked around and grinned. Then he beckoned to his workers. "Gather closely," he whispered. "I have something to show you."

With his teeth, he tugged at the bandages and began to unwind them. Some of the men moved back as the red color deepened on the long strips that rolled off Lee Jim's hands. But when he got to the end, there were his baby fingers, still attached to his hands, as pink and healthy as any man's!

Afterword

The Chinese have been in North America for over one hundred and forty years, but even today they are seen as foreigners and newcomers. This is unfortunate, because they have played a major role in helping to transform the west coast of this continent.

I invented the stories in this book. But they are all firmly rooted in real places and events, in things such as the work world of the Chinese, the folk traditions they brought from China, and the frontier society of this continent. Some of these things I recalled from growing up in Chinatown, listening to stories and overhearing adult conversations. Other things I discovered from research and reading.

These stories came out of my work in Canadian history, but they are part of the American past, too, because the Chinese in Canada and the United States shared many experiences. In both countries gold rushes in the nineteenth century attracted the first Chinese from the village regions of south China (to the Chinese, North America became popularly known as Gold Mountain). In both countries Chinese laborers helped build transcontinental railways. In both countries they worked in primary industries such as salmon canning, farming, and lumbering. And in both countries anti-Chinese laws were passed to block their immigration, and racial hostility forced them to live and work in Chinatowns, away from the rest of the population.

History is more than old dates and dusty numbers. In North America, the Chinese struggled through decades of hard times, where the memories are so sad and bitter that many want to forget them. But we shouldn't forget, because there are other memories that are rich and full, and it is this combined experience that has shaped who we have become.

I hope these stories will carve a place in the North American imagination for the many generations of Chinese who have settled here as Canadians and Americans, and help them stake their claim to be known as pioneers, too.

Paul Yee
Toronto, 1989